TIMES SQ

BROADWAY

W 45 ST

GEORGE ABBOTT
WAY

NO
TURN

NO
TURN

Larry Gets Lost
in
New York City

Illustrated by John Skewes
Written by Michael Mullin and John Skewes

little bigfoot
an imprint of sasquatch books
seattle, wa

Manufactured in China by C&C Offset Printing Co. Ltd. Shenzhen, Guangdong Province, in September 2016

Published by Little Bigfoot, an imprint of Sasquatch Books
18 17 16   15 14 13 12 11 10 9 8 7

Book design by Mint Design

Library of Congress Cataloging-in-Publication Data

Mullin, Michael.
  Larry gets lost in New York City / illustrations by John Skewes ; written by Michael Mullin and John Skewes.
     p. cm.
  ISBN 978-1-57061-620-4
1. New York (N.Y.)--Juvenile literature. 2. New York (N.Y.)--Description and travel--Juvenile literature. 3. Historic buildings--New York (State)--New York--Juvenile literature. 4. Historic sites--New York (State)--New York--Juvenile literature. 5. New York (N.Y.)--Buildings, structures, etc.--Juvenile literature. I. Skewes, John. II. Title.
  F128.33.M85 2010
  974.7´1--dc22
                              2009039496

Larry adopts a food bank in every city he visits. A portion of the proceeds from this book will be donated to the Food Bank for New York City. Visit it at foodbanknyc.org.

www.larrygetslost.com

SASQUATCH BOOKS
1904 Third Avenue, Suite 710
Seattle, WA 98101
(206) 467-4300

www.sasquatchbooks.com
custserv@sasquatchbooks.com

This is **Larry.**   This is **Pete.**
In the back of a taxi they ride down the street.

Their yellow cab **beeped**
As it made its way
Toward another adventurous,
City-filled day.

This one was by far
The **biggest** they'd seen,
An island and mainland
With bridges between!

They got out of the cab on a bustling street.
Lots of neckties and cell phones and fast-moving feet.

It seems all were thinking about money to spend
To make sense of it all, Larry asked a new friend.

In a new neighborhood, they made their next stop,
Full of bookstores and galleries, restaurants and shops.

WALL STREET
Named for a wall that used to stand at the city's edge, this is where traders met in the 1800s.

GREENWICH VILLAGE
One of New York's oldest and liveliest neighborhoods, Greenwich Village is home to Washington Square Park.

Construction in New York City goes as deep underground as it does high in the sky.

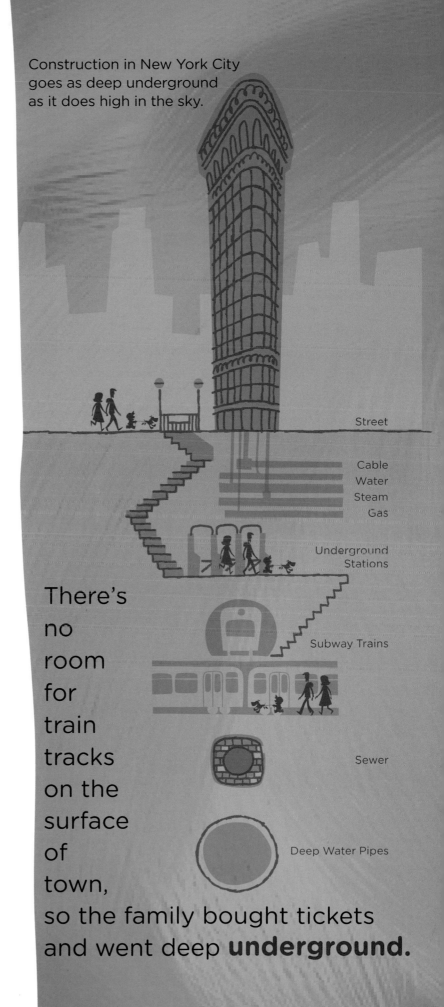

Street

Cable
Water
Steam
Gas

Underground Stations

Subway Trains

Sewer

Deep Water Pipes

There's no room for train tracks on the surface of town, so the family bought tickets and went deep **underground.**

From the train Larry lunged for a triangle-shaped snack,
Quite sure he could eat it in time to get back.

He grabbed it and chomped, sending cheese in the air.
Then he heard a loud **WHOOOOOSH!!!!!**

. . . And saw Pete wasn't there.

To begin his search,
Larry went **up, up, up.**
Such a very long staircase
For a little lost pup.

A huge station appeared
At the top of his climb,
Where a shiny round **clock**
Kept the people on time.

GRAND CENTRAL TERMINAL
Usually called Grand Central
Station, it has more platforms than
any train station in the world. More
than 100,000 people pass through
every day.

Once outside, he ran
In a wandering line
Past fluttering flags,
Each a different design.

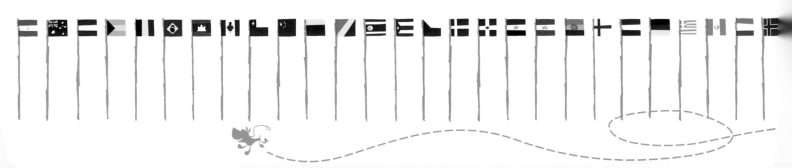

UNITED NATIONS BUILDING
The United Nations was started in 1945 to promote world peace. More than 190 countries are members, each with its flag flying out in front of the U.N. Headquarters.

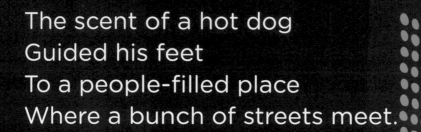

The scent of a hot dog
Guided his feet
To a people-filled place
Where a bunch of streets meet.

Cars stopping at red lights,
Then **zooming** on green,
The billboards and buildings
Were the **biggest** he'd seen.

The whole place seemed to Larry
Like a circus outside,
Or a honking-loud, blinking-light
CARNIVAL RIDE!

TIMES SQUARE
Sometimes called "The Crossroads of the World," it's shaped
more like a triangle. Times Square is named after the old New
York Times Building.

It was so hard to leave
This exciting square,
But he had to; he could see
That Pete wasn't there.

THE BRONX

YANKEE STADIUM

YANKEE STADIUM
The New York Yankees have won 27 championships, more than any other sports team.

All through New York,
Larry looked high and low.
Where could Pete be?
Where on earth did he go?

The family went uptown
On train number **4**,
To a big baseball place
Where they heard a crowd roar.

Meanwhile, Larry wondered about a building he'd found. People called it a "square" even though it was **ROUND.**

MADISON SQUARE GARDEN
"The Garden" is the home of the Rangers hockey team and the Knicks and Liberty basketball teams.

NEW YORK CITY SUBWAY SYSTEM
New York City has one of the oldest and busiest public transportation systems in the world, with more than 600 miles of track and more than 6,000 subway cars.

The **PURPLE** line took
Pete, Mom, and Dad to a place
Where they saw a big **planet**
And **rockets for space.**

They went south on the Q train,
But just like before,
There was no sign of Larry
At this place by the shore.

CONEY ISLAND
Families have played in the sun at this beach for
more than 100 years, even before the boardwalk
was built in 1923.

BROOKLYN

FLUSHING MEADOWS CORONA PARK
The Unisphere, made from solid steel for the 1964 World's Fair, is 140 feet tall.
The New York Hall of Science and the New York Mets' Citi Field are next door.

7

Thinking of Pete, Larry stayed on the hunt,
And passed a great building with a **fountain** out front.
People walked in, dressed-up, looking smart.
Inside, a performance was ready to start.

LINCOLN CENTER FOR THE PERFORMING ARTS
Lincoln Center is home to the Metropolitan Opera, the New York
Philharmonic, and the New York City Ballet.

Larry then found a ship
That could not be ignored.
So big and so mighty
With a **museum** on board!

INTREPID

He ran 'round in **circles,**

Other cool vessels
Caught Larry's eye,
One for **deep** water
And some for the **sky.**

INTREPID SEA, AIR & SPACE MUSEUM
The museum is home to an aircraft carrier, a
submarine, a destroyer, and 30 aircraft.

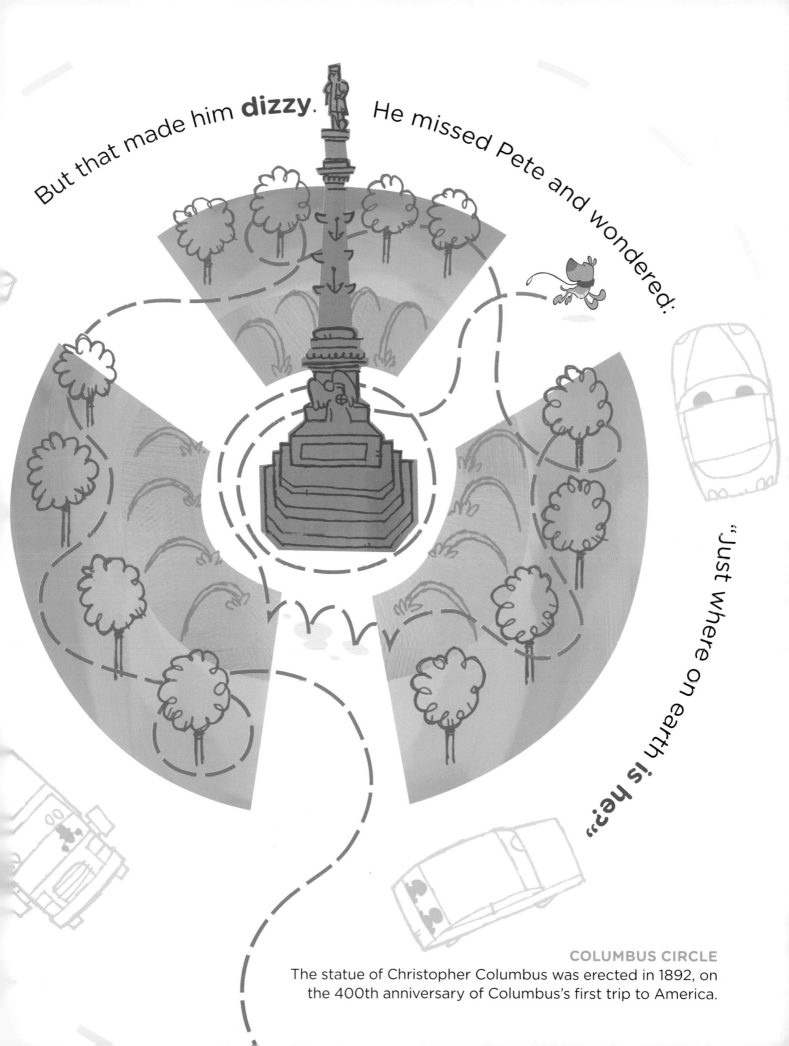

But that made him **dizzy**. He missed Pete and wondered:

"Just where on earth is he?"

COLUMBUS CIRCLE
The statue of Christopher Columbus was erected in 1892, on the 400th anniversary of Columbus's first trip to America.

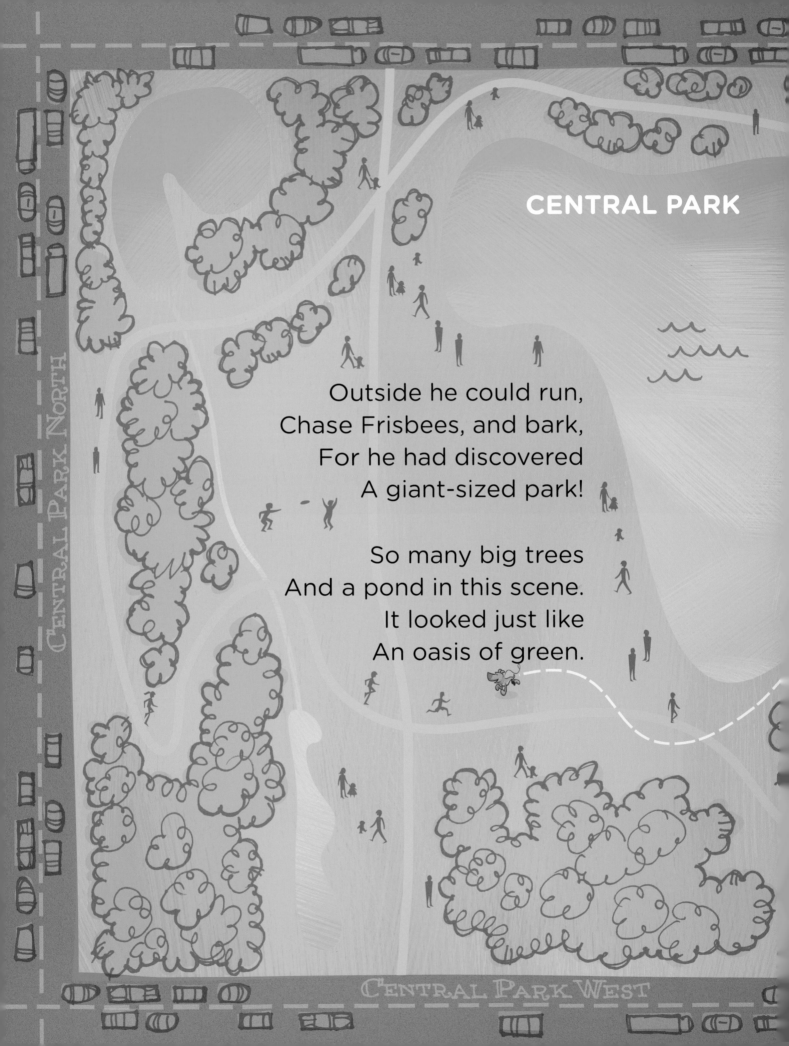

CENTRAL PARK

Outside he could run,
Chase Frisbees, and bark,
For he had discovered
A giant-sized park!

So many big trees
And a pond in this scene.
It looked just like
An oasis of green.

CENTRAL PARK SOUTH

Step after step, up a mountain he climbed.
This place looked important. Could Pete be inside?

THE METROPOLITAN MUSEUM OF ART
"The Met" has a collection of more than 2 million works of
art, from ancient Roman armor to American modern art.

In another museum
Larry had quite a scare.
He was lost, but **this monster**
Did not seem to care.

THE AMERICAN MUSEUM OF NATURAL HISTORY
The collection has more than 32 million specimens, including
real dinosaur skeletons and a full-size model of a whale.

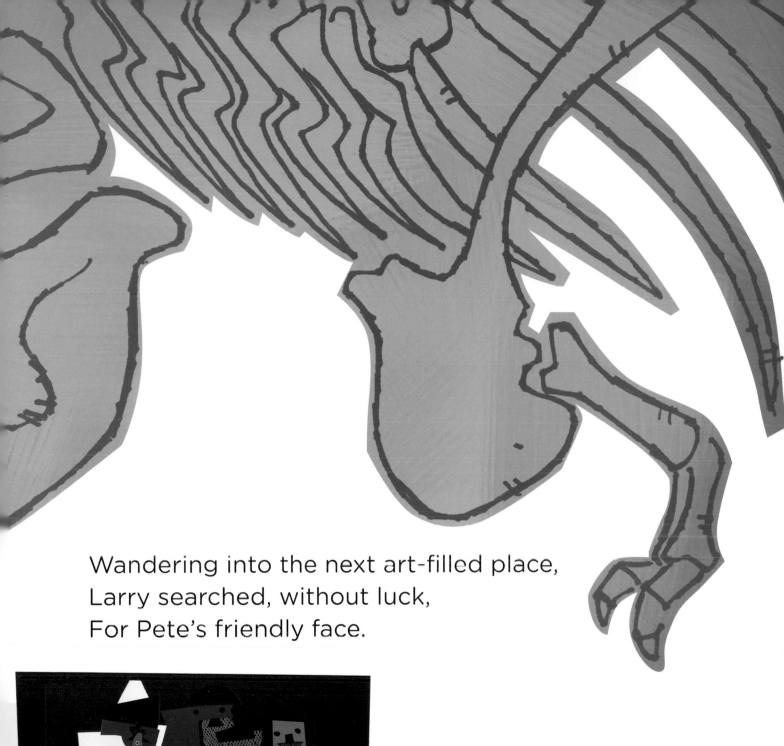

Wandering into the next art-filled place,
Larry searched, without luck,
For Pete's friendly face.

THE MUSEUM OF MODERN ART (MoMA)
MoMA shows modern art of all kinds:
paintings, sculptures, movies, furniture—
even a real helicopter.

Then back in the city
He saw beautiful sights—
Buildings and **sculptures**
All shiny and bright.

ROCKEFELLER CENTER
Every winter the plaza is turned into a frozen pond for ice
skaters and decorated with a lighted Christmas tree.

He saw a young girl
Tying her laces.
Larry gave her one of his
"I'm lost, help me" faces.

Her mom patted his head
And checked his ID.
"Now I'll find Pete,"
Larry thought,
"Lucky me!"

RADIO CITY MUSIC HALL
Radio City is the largest indoor theater in the
world. Its marquee is as long as a city block.

And find him he did with the help of that pair.
The whole family **was way, way** far up in the air.

He was so glad to have that tag 'round his neck
As he hugged Pete on the building's famous roof deck.

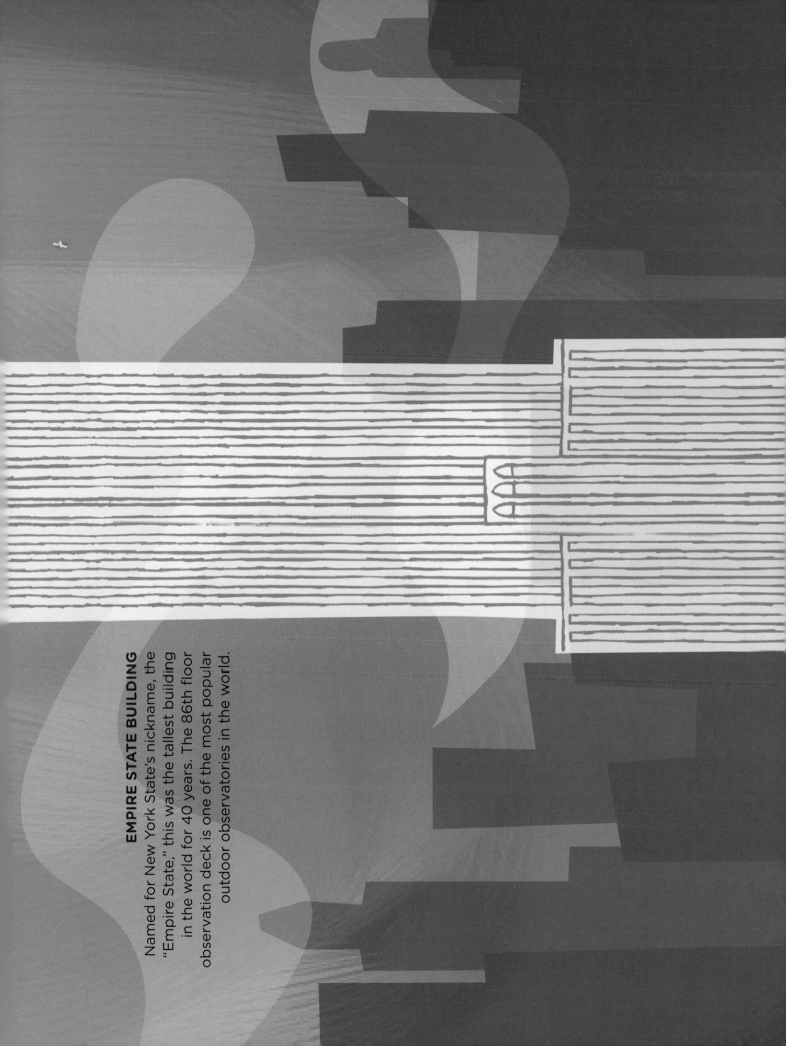

EMPIRE STATE BUILDING

Named for New York State's nickname, the "Empire State," this was the tallest building in the world for 40 years. The 86th floor observation deck is one of the most popular outdoor observatories in the world.

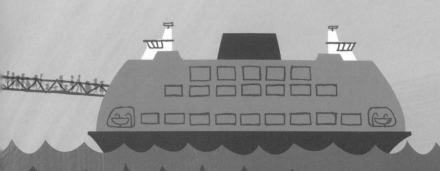

As the sun sank lower
In the city sky,
A big green lady
Waved them **goodbye**.

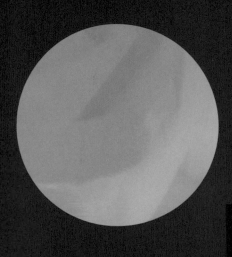

STATEN ISLAND FERRY
The ferry runs 24 hours a day, 7 days a week. On an average day, the boats carry 65,000 passengers—more than 20 million a year!

STATUE OF LIBERTY
Lady Liberty stands on her own little island in New York Harbor. Her torch reaches 305 feet into the air.

Larry and Pete
Fell asleep right away.
It had been an exciting
Exhausting day.

Get More Out of This Book

The City That Never Sleeps

New York is a loud, busy, and bustling city. After the first reading of the book, read through it a second time and have students point out words or pictures that demonstrate the hustle-and-bustle of New York. (Text examples: fast-moving feet, honking-loud, zooming. Illustration examples: Times Square, Yankee Stadium.) Do students think it would be exciting or exhausting to live in New York?

Imaginary Field Trip!

How many students have visited New York? As a class, using the book for reference, make a list of reasons why it would be a great destination for a class trip. How would the class travel there? What sites would they be most interested in seeing? What attraction or landmark would they want the hotel to be near?

Job Interview

Many, many people work in New York. Can students name some New York jobs, or job possibilities, that they spotted during the reading? (Examples: policeman on horse-back, taxi driver, hot-dog vendor, baseball player.) Have students dictate or write about the type of job they would imagine having if they lived there.

Signs of the Times

Have students draw their own Times Square billboard advertising their favorite New York place, landmark, or sports team.

TEACHER'S GUIDE: The above discussion questions and activities are from our teacher's guide, which is aligned to the Common Core State Standards for English Language Arts for Grades K to 1. For the complete guide and a list of the exact standards it aligns with, visit our website: SasquatchBooks.com